Debriefing the Rose

Also by Mary di Michele

Stranger in You: Selected Poems and New
Under My Skin (novel)
Luminous Emergencies
Immune to Gravity
Necessary Sugar
Anything is Possible (editor)
Mimosa and Other Poems
Bread and Chocolate
Tree of August

Debriefing the Rose

Poems

Mary di Michele

Anansi

Published in 1998 by
House of Anansi Press Limited
34 Lesmill Road, Toronto, ON
Canada   M3B 2T6

Distributed in Canada by
General Distribution Services Inc.
30 Lesmill Road
Toronto, Canada   M3B 2T6
Tel. (416) 445-3333
Fax (416) 445-5967
e-mail: Customer.Service@ccmailgw.genpub.com

02 01 00 99 98   1 2 3 4 5

Canadian Cataloguing in Publication Data

di Michele, Mary, 1949-
Debriefing the rose

Poems.
ISBN 0-88784-623-8

I. Title.

PS8557.I55D42 1998   C811'.54   C98-930772-7
PR9199.3.D55D42 1998

Cover art: Pekoe Jones
Printed and bound in Canada
Typesetting: ECW Type & Art, Oakville

*House of Anansi Press gratefully acknowledges the
Canada Council for the Arts and the Ontario Arts Council
for their support of our publishing program.*

for Kleis

Contents

It was granted to me to discard the authority of the rose.
— Leonard Cohen

A rose is a rose is a rose
— Gertrude Stein

I

Walking on the Mirror

What Is Desire?

      Love. When I sit beside my
lover at dinner and glance down at his jeans
where the fabric forms a loose pocket
at the thigh and the muscle tenses as I touch
him and he turns to me and this is familiar
and I know him with my mouth and my cheek where
it rested the night before and with any language
which must refer to the body,
thigh, buttocks, penis, hand,
and mouth, *la bouche, la bocca,*
or ear, *l'oreille, l'orecchio* where I enter

him and he listens with my

tongue. This alone
is completion,
                desire meeting desire

in that tango of fabric and flesh.

ii

Loss. The moment
I learned my lover's desire was

                                    not

for my self I did nothing:

when he helped me move into my new apart
ment, to motivate himself he played
a game — with each glass he unwrapped
he undressed another woman.
He dropped one,
                    me,

and then there was no

                    one to sweep up the splinters,

the bro

                ke   n

                            b

                it

                        s

            .

iii

'Not love.' Or other complications, an etiquette
of when to come and when to quit. A *rendezvous,*
a meet me at happy hour for cocktails.
                                        Yours
for martinis and eternity
                        for an hour.

You can't sleep in a strange bed, but was it
sleep you came for?
                        Indeed, *mon semblable,*
the slumber of the mind when the skin is wide
awake. How quaint! You read Baudelaire

to the man because you're restless, not
Les Fleurs du Mal, not those syllables,
                                        distilled,
taken by the spoonful, a cherry-flavoured syrup,
but *quelques petites poèmes en prose.* Their

irony and slapstick suit him best. His style of white silk
gloves gobbling up the rent. Oh Charles, what's
love without the knot

                        in the throat? The single
straw through which a man slurps up several
pink ladies? Because it's two
                        for the price of one
you can afford to drink, to
                        drink to be drunk.

Poem Not Written by Diane Arbus

See that man in the photo, the one
in the beige shorts, the red shirt,
the one walking away
from the camera, tell him to turn
around, tell him that the woman taking
the photo loves him. The DO NOT ENTER
sign in the foreground
is not significant. The ONE WAY
pointing in another direction
is not significant. They're street signs.

It's true our photographer has no eye
for any landscape outside
the body. She loves. Hell
our photographer is no poet with a Pentax,
no Arbus with a Leica whose people appear
like metaphors. Invented.
This scene is plodding, literal, pedestrian.
It is dull, it is droll — her lack
of perspective.
                        But imagine instead
the man in the beige shorts riding
off into the sunset, the Grand Canyon, the Gobi
desert, and it begins
to get interesting. He's on a horse.
You all know how to read that.

But no, there's not a tell-tale
mark, the legs of the man are blank.
The street scene eludes deeper
interpretation. It's all urban grid.

This photo tells you nothing
more. The photographer records as
if there were another reason.

To you the man is a stranger.
He must be thirsty, he is hurrying
to what looks like the nearest bar.
Or imagine he is Jack, "The Marked Man,"
the woman has promised to marry him
if he will erase his tattoos. He is rushing
to the parlour where he is written.

Poem Beginning with a Line by Roberto Juarroz

There are clothes that last longer than love
stored in a trunk, the dress he divorced
me in was white too but embroidered
in the bright colours of Easter
eggs. It was spring then,
I was younger, there's a photo
where I'm wearing this dress and smiling
the way we do for the camera and occasions.
Without sincerity. My skin
was better, was different, well you see
the light used to linger in it and that
created an aura of beauty you will miss
with ordinary looking. But my allure
was tenuous, friable, its texture
more pollen than petal
of the corolla, its blossom
dead, desiccated in the vase
by which he paused, his fingers not
touching, debriefing the rose
is such a common flower, more cliché
than symbol for love and the brevity
of pleasure. Now the child is more than
half-grown. The miracle, the dress eludes
moths through disuse, escaped from
disease if not estrangement. I do
not understand how anyone could remember
such insignificant details, a Mexican wedding
dress, an overblown posy, not
its scent, its story, it's still sorry
for a thousand and one untold nights.

A Bouquet of Rapini

Eating is touch carried to the bitter end.

i

The vegetable is bitter green
                     and full of *vite*
amens, the iron I
              need, my blood
tired from a hole
              lotta loveless
ness and it's nicely
              wrapped as if it were a
gift and it is
              my trophy, it has real weight
this bouquet, but the
              man, the wished-for
end to a long line of men
offers me something fresh, something nourishing
he fills me up with much more than the daily
recommended ferrous sulphate and folic acid.

ii

You know romance is roses
but perhaps the pattern on the paper
is not
        what's inside.

iii

No, it's not
                flowers he brings me
what I need
                his body, his bloody
                                rapini, the scent of rain in tin

cans is better for my health and he's so
good to me I'm surprised when he won't
stay to dine because his taste is for
alone, doesn't need my company, just breathing

room and the men-

iv

u's planned for one,
                        he's gone
for good this time.
                        O woman starved,
O woman buy your own
                        (it's not so dear)

rapini for $2.50 a small bunch
at *le Faubourg*. But when he pays
no price
            is too high.

I'm good

v

Steam rapini or drop into a few inches of salted, rapidly boiling water until tender. They turn a neon green. Heat olive oil, extra virgin, cold pressed, gently in a frying pan. Sliver cloves of garlic, many, and cook until golden, along with some red dried chili peppers. Drop the steamed rapini into the oil and stir fry. May be served as a side dish or on top of pasta along with some ricotta cheese you simply warm in the pan with the rapini for a minute or two.

vi

                                    at pumping irony.
Away from him this strength is new, I lie

alone in bed and like it.
Observe these arms are winter
                    white and the biceps

are taut, are long
                    lean and feline. The lynx,

before it devours the inner child,
                    as it crouches to spring

or settles to sleep
                curled under snow.

Choosing Gifts for Women Friends,
Their Long Hair

Choosing gifts for my women friends from the stall
of a street vendor of ambiguous gender,
"Does she have hair, your friend?"
He questions me curiously I think
he sees Joan waiting for her fate in Rouen,
he sees Frida after Diego has left her.

For Sharon I choose a clip with cancan
angels, the beauty and the burlesque
of women dancing for show, for some
body else. I can visualize the French
roll she'll gather at the back where the girls
keep kicking up their heels. That dark
storm is her hair. Trouble trouble
on the double.

For Alice I choose a burnished bronze comb
with figures from dream time.
For some it's a relief to sleep
for a hundred years, for some
to wake is the curse.
The barrette is made in India
but her colouring is from the far
north where light is slant.
She rests, her hair a strain of winter
wheat, the grasshopper thinks she is food,
but the prince knows she is field.

For Roo I discover a hairclip in tones
chiaroscuro, silver and black gold
metal embossed with a collage
of creatures from the deep
because she is stranger
than seahorse, pregnant with secrets
neither male nor female
but both and the stars too

are fish, their fires
doused in ocean depths. And oh
the swaying branch of her hair
persuades Buddha to climb onto the back
of a tortoise. Reborn
to live in Ruth, nirvana is
                          nothing.

Earth, water, and turbulent
air, cut more wood for the
hearth, please, hydro
electric power is not
enough, you need them,
their lips to read these words.

My Hart Crane

*Language has built towers and bridges, but itself
  is inevitably as fluid as always.*

I

There are no stars tonight save
memory, there are no stars.
Tonight the body disappears.
No stars — the constellation Aries
is invisible, revised by the universe
of quasars and quarks. I stand on board a mere
marine vessel. Vision is a voyage. I feel
the rocking of waves, I feel
the deck bucking beneath my feet,
its worn wood. I have travelled back
nearly a century to the Caribbean
where it's still midnight, April 1932.

Slipping into Hart's shadow, we
see no stars tonight, even the sea
is clouded over, murky. This is an elegy
for all of us Harts who want to change,
who make pacts with suicide and chance
it with the stars. We channel, is it neurosis,
our leaping

                        into our fates? Murky. No moon,
no stars save memory. It's late, Dr. K, the sky
is murky tonight. The sea is rocking.
Its lullaby lures us from our berth
to a death somewhat cozier. There are no stars
the briny depths, a cistern of tears, a spittoon

for sharks yet I'd follow you without a second

                            thought through fathoms
I'd sink to stay put, in the past

                        with you, my beleaguered,
Hart. Whom have we abandoned
in the stateroom? Who expects us to come
back? The dark

cleft in the sky without
                    stars must be re-
remembered, the life
                       lines un-

ravelled.

Because you could not love your own
body, your man
                hood, your cover, your female
lover.
             Because I, because I

see no stars any night
               save memory.

II

Rapture/Rupture

The sun is also a star making us
blind to all others like bridesmaids
dimmed by the dazzle of the bride.
That was me before Hart started
on the booze at breakfast.

Call me Peg Might-Have-Been-Hart-
Crane who travelled to Mexico for a quick,
if not easy, divorce, but was waylaid
by love. I knew him already, he was
a friend of my husband's. But I never
knew the man who hit me. *Yes*, I cried,
Hart, you're a volcano! But I didn't expect
him to blow up in my face! How he could

singe me with a single word, though I never
minded because of the poetry, because
of his knack for making the language
sing! The art made everything all right
and that he was so oddly sensitive
writing verse as he cranked the music
full blast, but as for the town's church bells,
their clanging drove him crazy, he said,
sound's just noise when it's not composed,
he said, *compared with their holy racket,*
our ship's propellers played Pachelbel.

It was lunch time. I had a headache and Hart
showed up in my stateroom unshaven and still
in his pyjamas to apologize the way men like to
blame the woman. He lamented my
clumsiness. But I had the sympathy
of the doctor and no more tolerance for Hart's
moods. Clearly that morning his guilt sparked

his greed, he ate all my congealing breakfast.
In the pocket of his robe, a crumpled telegram,
an invitation to live without me in Chagrin
Falls, Ohio. Happily, though his mother was dead,
his father's wife was most welcoming.

Bankers and brokers are believed
to jump for less
                    or is it more? I get
mixed up easily, but I do know when the right
side is wrong you're driving
                    in a foreign country.

Like what Hart made of my boyish figure
attached to his mother's face. He was no
lover of falsetto but his grandmother was the
only woman he truly cherished. Her will,
a trunk full of love letters, left him a poet's
legacy, while his mother's divorce left him

bankrupt. Bankers and brokers,
like those who were believed
to have jumped for less
                    or was it more?

III

A Boy's Love for His Mother

That hate is but the vengeance of a long caress.

Even if she had been the real Gioconda
she deserved that moustache. My mother,
how I remember her, Grace
Hart Crane. Without the Grace
she was myself. Without the Grace
she was the unguent, she was the grease
my sailor would smear on his penis
before he slipped it into her baby,

Hart. It was never Peg I loved nor
mother nor the sea I sang in weary tropes.
It was another drowning I preferred
down in the boiler room with my sailor.

At noon the deck broiled with impossible
heat. That She
also burned at night was my fault I suppose
her hand might have been put to better
use, but she had to light that damn cigarette
herself. Bang! Bang! the Cuban

cigars exploded, a clumsy, a careless
accident and not my concern except
for the rude fact that someone so
small could stumble so
stupidly was all I thought there was to be
said about that unpleasant surprise.

But we fell, together, in love in Mexico
where She was divorcing another
man for less. Not that I
was drunk, not that I

had never been engaged before
more happily to the bottle
than to another woman. She didn't

want to forgive me. She complained
about a "headache" though She
endured the din, the clamouring
of all the bells in Mexico without

raising an eyebrow.
                    Why did I do it,
you still ask, now that you know Her story and are
no longer on my side?
                    Dear reader,
this is what upset me, for the first time
her distress seemed bigger than mine.

I didn't jump to punish Peg, I didn't
jump to drown. The sea was so flat, so
still, its surface was pure mirror. I saw
birds, not fish, in the water, I saw wisps
of fair-weather cumulus drifting, not
sargassum. The sun below shone as brightly
as the sun above. It wasn't that I couldn't

swim but that I had never before aimed
so high. I didn't plunge to drown, I leapt

                              to fly.

IV

The Hour of Pan

It wasn't storm, it was calm.
It wasn't cold or midnight
as one might expect it was
hot and high noon. It was the hour

of Pan, of panic, when the shadow
has nowhere to go but back
into the self. And the water was not wine

dark, nor the glistening of iodine
on your Hart's lips with the grave
promise not delivered in Mexico.
No the sea was suicide

                        yellow on that day.

It seemed so beautiful, it seemed pure
radiance, all gold
                        as in a Turner canvas —
and on fire!

V

Walking on the Mirror

Their ship was the Orizaba, the sea,
the Caribbean.
                    At midnight,
alas, I had already missed him,
at midnight, he was no more alive
than when I first read his work and ventured
into the past, through this text, with language
as our only link, with language
as our talisman. Why is it that to find also
means to lose
                    the grail? The bridegroom
had been swept away, unwed, but
with the ring in his pocket. Left behind
was the fiancée, his widow in words
alone, smoking away her left-handed
sorrow. Into the sea she flicked

                    flaming ash.
Mary, you found not the man but his wake.
That winsome visage in the sea was the moon,
not me, and Peg's lament was directed to her own
reflection in the compact, to the pretty face
clouded with grief and powder. For a woman
the self must be portable in the purse and fulfil
the need to be made smaller by what she sees.
There was always too much woman in me and I in
None. Fancy pants, flit, fetishist, fruit, faggot,
finocchio — that was me, all fay-male!

"If sharks don't get the bloody fool
first — then the propellers'll make
mincemeat of the body." The body, the

definite article, not the man, not the
irrecoverable subject of the poem.

Christ could walk on water, but I believe,
not even He, without getting sucked
in, could have stepped on such a mirror,
a sea smooth as glass and as slippery,
the light at noon erasing all visible depth.

Self-Portrait 1994

Symmetry in the moth is to attract a mate.

Asymmetry in art is not
                        natural design
not reproduction.

What's interesting if not beautiful's
                                    mismatched, unmarried.
Regard the face, the right brow is
                            perfectly smooth,
while the left unfurls like a fan
                        no, with something of the masculine,
the cock's comb
                    its ragged red end.

Ambiguity in shades of blue or green
                                whether sea or weed
the eyes in the mirror look
                            to the silver backing.
The lips are parted as if
                        to speak silence. The right

side is scarred, an accident, a bad
stitch job. The jaw
is squared, the cheekbones
                            in love with line.
The generous nose is fleshy, full,
                            born to gorge

on fragrance, hothouse odour of rose
pales before the kitchen smells of rice, risotto,
of basil, olive oil and garlic.

Now the face hides in the hands
                    which belong to the Father.
Now the mouth opens to sing
                    an aria from *La Traviata*.
She is less mother
                    than sibling or progeny.
She is less teacher
                    than disciple or novice.
She is less writer
                    than finger tracing
what it means to be
                    blue in Braille.

The poet turns away from the page, the pulsing
                                        cursor,
the WordPerfect, and opens the door
to the reader
            who is her true lover.

"I've missed you, I've missed you so . . ."

II

R.S.V.P.

Répondez s'il vous plaît

Invitation to Read Wang Wei
in a Montréal Snowstorm

In middle age I'm beyond asking or waiting to be asked, that river I've stepped into more than twice: love, sex, marriage and all that razzmatazz. With the ringer on the phone turned off, there are no more *mauvais numéros*. So in tranquillity I can sit on the couch the cat uses as a scratching board and feel the shredded fabric rough against my calves. The TV remote won't work without batteries. Surprise, surprise. Just as well, when the electronic screen is mute I can perceive a subtler illumination emanating from all things.

Wavering with winter trees, as if written in Chinese characters, black ink strokes on a white and blowing page; in the swirling storm, I too might be drawn to mean something.

Woowoo . . . woowoo . . . whistling of the dead. Pipe organ playing in the deconstructed cathedral.

During the Tang dynasty, on the Asian continent, thirteen hundred years ago, a question was posed for which we still hope for an answer: "How do you succeed or fail in life?" Wang Wei answered his friend, the sub-prefect Zhang, with an image: "A fisherman's song is deep in the river."

Wei, I have learned to excel through too much effort and a job in government service. Does it look like winning to you, the car in the driveway, the terra-cotta coloured cottage? When what I long for most is to sit and listen to song on your river estate? In the thick of the buzzing gnats of summer I have observed old men by the Lachine rapids drop worms from their lines. Though no fish were caught, the men snared clouds on their hooks.

Do I dare to step outside now, in the new year, into the frigid garden, into the blizzard that makes hair white; do I dare to sink into snow, thigh deep? The light numinous. The night luminous, I plough a way through drifts to the back of the house. The wind unwrapping my scarf, an anti-mother, a father who's just blown into town from the northwest for the weekend.

27

Why do I bother to ask Wei, with no hope of another answer? What, on any night, can be seen through a dark window into a darkened house? When the storm subsides, when it's calm again, I'll catch the moon reclining in an armchair. She who reads by her own light.

Invitations to Perfume

i

The mode in which perfume moves across the room is familiar music. Without the words. Mmmmmmmm you hum, lalala lala, though you can't remember a line, the melody haunts, hints at an experience you've missed, names a demon lover without a face.

Mmmmmmmmmmm the melody waits at the entrance to an amphitheatre. When you twist the top open all the way, your eau de Cologne, the volume amplifies into a muted thunder.

Dolby of musk and white flowers.

Or, if you prefer, tune to notes in the faintest ghost of amber. That's the ghost of a ghost. Though dead, these continue to breathe in oil.

More incantation than distillation. It makes you hyperventilate, feel heady, weak, as on a honeymoon, with that longing for which you've had more than your fill.

ii

The mode in which flowers disclose themselves through fragrance is a fine art. When you are told the Dance Master is soon to be married, your mouth opens. But to respond requires crushing so many tons of rose petals to produce an ounce of attar. Joy, much, much . . . for someone else. It's an art like music. A scent, a song, a soupçon of story. Cork it. Store it. In no, in little time, this too will be stale.

Invitation to Death by Carbon Monoxide Poisoning

A colourless, odourless gas, a drifting, a numbing as with snow but without the cold, an easeful death. Half in love with it. No, not that, not love, but what's left of it, the traces. As from red wine, the tannins.

You wake in the middle of the night, the bed a carousel, the first alert alarm sounding. You go to the window, but it is sealed shut, the ice of November, December and January. You try another window and another. You get out the WD-40 but you can only spray the inside of the frame. Now you have the chemical smell, the oily film on your fingers, but no fresh air. You go to the front door and breathe briefly through the mail slot. The night air a missive, the night air an unsolicited letter from him, a postcard from some exotic place on the other side of the world where you've never been. You'll never be. Be again with him.

Your lungs test the air, a polar bath. A bathos. You step back, secure the slot. Let nothing from him ever push its way through to you again. You go back upstairs because you are tired of interruptions and no other form of sleep could be long or satisfying enough.

Invitation to the Funeral

Not in black, you dress in pink, a silk dress, the rose of morning or evening, uncertain, whether its hue is about to intensify or clarify. When arriving and departing are drawn as simultaneous actions. When a woman watches her husband at the door leaving for work for the second time that day, suitcase in hand, that pink drains from her cheeks to resurface in her eyes.

Definitely not in black, not in that vampire cloak where all light is sucked up, swallowed down, drained entirely. You dress in pink. When a friend dies, even such a one whose laughter was unquenchable, whose laughter would illuminate the darkened theatre where you were to meet, even such a one whom you thought you could never lose, whose laughter gurgled spontaneously in your own throat, even such a close companion in death slips back into a formality which stiffens you with strangeness. The eulogy will introduce you to her as if for the first time.

Weren't you embarrassed, in public, by such a display, her belly laughs, such a raucous display? In the simian circle of the petting zoo, the crowd threw peanuts. Children recognized her as one of them!

The incense is scented myrrh, not cherry blossom, though it's spring. A Catholic funeral, your friend seems to have regressed, reneged on her secular life; your friend has made a Rimbaudian confession. Though another poet wrote that each man may carry within him a dose of natural opiates, she was a woman and that dose must have been halved. She relied on soft drugs, caffeine or cognac, in demitasse, after dinner. Her fingers were stained, not with nicotine, but with carotene; opium of pumpkin, yam, and carrot.

Her dying wish was to be cremated in an open coffin; the intense heat raising the cadaver so she would sit up one last time among friends. Her hair, a blazing aura. But by law the body does not belong to the dead, it is owned by its natural heirs, the living family.

Now her laughter rattles in my mind as if it were merely punctuation for a sitcom. It is definitely not the staccato song she churred in life, not the pizzicato of her pleasure.

She has become the most obscure object of your desire. At the open coffin you look into a mirror. A pink silk dress, pretty, proper, if dusty from the back of the closet, not the black leggings in which she lived and died. A cover-girl face, a corsage of camellias, and a paperback book (it would have burned well) for the journey, some easy reading, the kind you reserve for airports and waiting rooms.

Invitation to the DNA Zoo

The body is a crowded zoo. In the *Jardin des Plantes*,
Paris, 1907, as if from behind bars, the poet
paces along with the panther, following its inward
spiral until, arriving at the centre of the cage, he

disappears. Angels in the aviary.
Under the skin there is fur.
Under the skin there is another
skin, a coat, lined in red
mink. Listen.

What is it? Simian or snake or something in
between, mewling in the spine?

Invitation to a Recessive Gene

In Latin blood legend traces the wolf.
In us instinct is not extinct, it's latent.
When the moon is full, the wolf.
Start running.

What yelps in you?

Invitation to Accidental Green

The French, *il fait beau*, seems right to describe the weather today; it makes beautiful, yes, makes, but what makes it so? Sun, sky, trees flashing their leaves in flaming primary colours. There's the luminosity of endings, the last frame in a film before the screen goes dark and the red house-lights come on, as, attempting to leave while the credits are running, you stumble over your neighbour's feet.

There's colour, brilliant colour, but there's something cosmetic about it, the corpse so beautifully made up she seems more ready to dance than to be buried. Indian summer some call it, the heat, the light,

> a match flaring up
> before it burns out.

The intensity of tones seems artificial, as if the green of the lawn were newly achieved by smudging sun in sky. The universe has its own palette like any child's; with the freshness of play, spilling over the lines in the colouring book, grass is replicated by running blue legs into the yellow dog. Accidental green like the first organic life on the planet. In the park you think this is a harmony no one else sees and coincidentally, no one else is there. The park is strangely deserted, depopulated, post–neutron bomb.

Where you sit is the centre. You stretch out, a strange border for the more delicate flowers. Your marigold sweater is what keeps insects away from the black tulips,

> blue dahlias . . . you dream
> > because someone dreamed
> before you.

Although they don't give off a scent, you can imagine how they speed up the sinuses, their black and gold pollen, a cheap and tainted form of cocaine. Cut by the bee.

If the be-all and end-all of all things is money or the pursuit of happiness for which you need money, then the first man you see today, making his way toward you with his hat in his hand, has to beg to get there. You keep change in your pockets for just such occasions, when it seems imprudent to open your purse. But he doesn't want anything from you, he uses his cap to brush away dead leaves so he can bask by the pedestal of an angel who's been

> awarded wings
>
>   and the droppings
> of pigeons.

"What a glorious day! They say it hasn't been this mild in a century. Too bad there's nobody here to enjoy it," he looks pointedly at you.

La Benvenuta

Rose, oh reiner Widerspruch, Lust,
Niemandes Schlaf zu sein unter soviel
Lidern

i

It's almost light when I stumble off the milk run from the south, at Montefalcone station. I drink in the dawn through spiced *caffe con latte*, a horizon foaming cinnamon. From the small café it's easy to catch a fast cab for Duino. Where you can unwind in the stillness of a village holding its breath. Moving into the 21st century, something slow! Something to surprise you with familiarity!

What? This mecca is a mere suburb, in the brochure described as "a little interlude of past elegance and charm away from the pressures of life today":

　　　　　 – 600 metres from the nearest motorway,
　　　　　 – 20 km. from Trieste,

a dormitory of geometric lawns, parallel streets, stucco walls and roses, roses opening reluctantly like eyes from dream-filled sleep, yes, fluttering petals like sticky eyelids over no 'I.'

ii

Cemetery from *koimeterion*, the Greek for sleeping chamber, from *koiman*, to put to sleep, related to the Latin, *cunae*, cradle.

There are cities built on cities in each word. There are cites
archaeological in each mote, in each compound,
in the suffix as in the pre
fix. Re
　　　　pose, I sleep, you sleep, she, we all
in time slip into that under
　　　　　　　world.

37

I slept, you slept, together we did
not sleep ever.

iii

Like melody in music there is no meaning in the text
without playing the words. Rilke, perpetually entering
without arriving, concert tickets in his pockets, attuned

to the instrument he most feared because *a person's life could be
ruined if, even in passing, he happened to hear a violin, and that tone
deflected his entire will to a denser fate.*

not to music, but to silence, its notation
in the sea-gull's cry, in the surge of surf,

you see, I have not arrived at music yet, but I know about sounds.

iv

Duino, doo-ee-no, a bird's call, doo-wee-know, a name un-
answerable in any language that is not bird.

The pulp of a first word, an unknown vocabulary, on the
tongue.

O the insanity of language: empty sign. Would you buy a
carton with EGGS printed on it but nothing inside? The irony is
if you're hungry you will pick it up even if you know it's empty.
It weighs

less than nothing, but summons
for you the oily gold of yolk, the sun
in a cloud of albumin.

v

Though I am just thinking of myself and what I might eat for breakfast, Rilke welcomes me. I feel rude for having read all his letters without writing back.

The other one, my body-, not my soul-, mate responds little:

he's rude or, worse, insensitive,
unmoved by the daily epistles
I pen, I pine for his reply,
my *love, love, love* criss-
crossed with *x*'s and *o*'s
while he signs a postcard
simply **il Magnifico.**

On his deathbed Rilke refused an appointment to the German academy. Born in Bohemia, language failed to make him German enough. Though the angel spoke to him in *Deutsch*, Rilke, seeking what was untranslatable, sometimes wrote in *français*.

After all wasn't it the French, Rodin and Cézanne, who taught him how to look at things? Through words it is too hard to get to the palpable world. In Paris he learned to pray differently.

O for a palette thick with paint,
O for the molten bronze of casting.

Before the French he did not know how to see although he made do with vision. Before cubism he had to form himself entirely from the inside out.

vi

In a letter to the Princess Maria, Rilke wrote words are
windows, *not to the world, but to infinity, yes to infinity.*

> But without words, the greater mystery's
> in silence, not as when the concert
> ends though the body continues
>
> vibrating, but as when the instrument,
> locked up in its case, can't be
> touched. In this manner the dead
>
> compose most deeply. Their notes
> slower than music to arrive.

vii

Although Rilke could not wait for *La Benvenuta* to respond
to his letters, he could wait to write poetry.

> *For every kiss you give me, darling, I'll give you three.*
>
> My notebook untouched, I kiss
> stationery, a lipstick script
> for **Il Magnifico**. If he will
> read these smeared lines.

*It has always been my custom to write to you on paper I normally
use for working.* But for this stranger, for this most welcome one,
for the woman who thanked him as her saviour, who said she
knew him as a friend, although he did not know her, for *La
Benvenuta* he reserved a higher element than onionskin. If his
reach had not exceeded his grasp he would have

> sky-written her name with a comet.

viii

Even though Magda von Hattingberg knew "The Stories of God," she could not know the thin man in his fortieth year who was estranged from his wife and child.

Rilke hoped for more than a reader's gratitude.

Her letters echoed Beethoven's word, the same syllables Rilke imagined hearing from the lips of the Sphinx:

Unpronounceable!

Yet when Rilke first saw the pockmarked stone of the enigma, the crush of bodies made the monumental seem commonplace to him. He had to come back in the night to truly listen.

For viewing, not the Sphinx, but the Venus Rising . . . in the Uffizi gallery, there are no after hours. I entered a room, crowded with tourists and experienced something similar, something very different. The gallery did not empty suddenly, my eyes did. In the presence of the Three Graces all else was absence. Such brilliant light radiated from the painting I had to shield my eyes. Blinded by a Botticelli from the fifteenth century more alive than I am today.

ix

To love a musician, a pianist, when you're tone deaf and unable to recall the simplest tune, is natural if you love absence, if you love silence and the sounds which define it, if you love all those things which you are not. So it was not unnatural for Rilke to court a woman whom he had never met, a woman who was already satisfied with him, who thanked him for a text written by a man he couldn't remember being. Did he hope that she could not be disappointed, she who already had what she wanted from him? And he — he was most happy in the writing to her!

But when writer met reader, he lost control. When reader met writer she found him paler than his pages. And the correspondence ended.

x

The castle has the air of a church filled with invisible presence. *Here is the angel, who doesn't exist, and the devil, who doesn't exist; and the human being, who does exist, stands between them, and (I can't help saying it) their unreality makes him more real to me.* More than he dreaded any devil, Rilke dreaded going home. In Clara's well-stocked cupboards, in rugs that needed beating, the visible world stalked. Chores made him feel unreal, ethereal.

When a writ found the scribe, even within the pristine portals of an Austrian dynasty, he was forced to deal with things, with accounts; his household goods were about to be auctioned off to pay the landlord in Paris.

That day the sea clouded over of its own accord, that day he was numbed by numbers to its beauty, the chiaroscuro, a sea silver with storm and light, the north wind raging. Completely absorbed in the business of composing a reply, he heard the angel of the elegies for the first time. He jotted down the angel's words in his notebook but ran inside to respond to his creditor.

xi

There was no way back from castle to cottage, no way home from royal mistress to wife, no way to hear the angel while living with his family, not above the din, not above the quotidian. Or so he thought. While as royalty's guest he could enter the chapel with its smells of incense and embalming fluids and feel more real than in the kitchen where Clara cooked every day another leek and potato soup.

Rilke's angel was not a guardian, but the terrible mother of death and beauty. His art demanded no family, it demanded a sex with fatal edges, a sword, which would shine for him most brightly. But only

in the distance. A brilliant
blade to be kept
            sheathed.

xii

In the *castello di Duino* several sabres, jewelled and orna-
mental, are displayed under glass.

Inside the tower is a staircase, spiral, scalloped. Some trade
in their real body for an empty vessel where the sea can sing more
fully, more truly; some can only listen from within the conch. At
the centre of the vortex I crouch. Waiting for the sea change.

There is a tap on my shoulder, an official directs me to rejoin
the other tourists, all German except for the lone housewife from
Trieste,

> *"Sei, Italiana?"*

xiii

Back to the present, to gardens filled with roses: you could
warm your hands by the red and yellow blooms. But there are
other hues which belong more properly to Rilke. With white and
ghostly blossoms strumming the trellis, I sense he would have
been more deeply in tune.

> O rose, many-petalled flower,
> flower feathered as if winged,
> soaring seraphim of scent, it was you
> who killed Rilke. Or so he claimed:
>
> dying Rilke admitted nothing, insisted
> his death was nobody's
> disease,

that it was his fate to succumb to a scratch from the thorn of a rose.

In the mind, memory has the power
of smell. Aromatic chronicles.
From each garden, from each cottage
gate, roses, their fragrance
blares all the way down to the cliffs
where the waves, weighty
enough to pound huge boulders
into pebbles, nevertheless fail to
mute that flower's scent. In the mind.

Il Magnifico is indifferent to poetry, to my missives from northern Italy. He sniffs the pillow, the sheets, for traces of my scent.

xv

Rilke was a poet who learned to mine riches from the unrequited:

Flowers to my right, in front of me as well, on the window ledge, too, flowers on the desk, on the table behind me, on the stool by the sofa, and all alone, on the mantelpiece, your red rose . . .

Il Magnifico sends no sign.

Don't think that I'm wooing.
Angel, and even if I were, you would not come.

xvi

Along the marine drive, strolling by a Porsche, by an Alfa Romeo, by a chameleon posing as a shrub. A man is painting a wrought-iron fence dark green. He rests on one knee as if he truly loves, as if he pleads to marry his job. It's not his fence, he's the hired man. Any stranger might guess from his frayed socks. Look where the back of his overalls rides up.

This is not my garden, house, or estate for that matter, nor the palace where I came in search of poetry, in search of its muse.

xvii

There's a wooded path, the *Sentiero Rilke,* following the cliffs. *Senti!* Listen! In Italian the angel of the elegies whispers, to listen is also a way to walk.

In the brochures *una passeggiata di sogno* is translated as "a pleasant walk in the Castle gardens with light refreshments." The morning moon is not the dreamer's, the morning moon shines for those who do not sleep, for those who do not deign to eat. Rilke, this dawning, you are more wan than I ever imagined.

In its setting, the moon seems to pause over the solitary balcony facing out to sea where Rilke would practise listening. In thundering tempest listening, for the angel, for the *sotto voce.*

> Below on the beach, below on what must be
> some private shore, a single white bikini
> glows.
>   Do you marvel to see the clothes
>
> when the woman's invisible?

xviii

What's mystery when it's all around? A home?

Though the sun burns in a cloudless sky, I'm huddled in a raincoat with the collar turned up. I ate some milk and fruit for supper nearly a century ago. Hunger makes me light-headed.

No, Rilke didn't wait to write, he waited for dictation.

> *Let such a person go out to his daily work, where*
> *greatness is lying in ambush . . .*

What rooted, what stubborn Romanticism makes me still believe I won't understand Rilke unless it storms, I won't understand what shook him in view of this

> serene and glistening sea. Rilke in storm
> finding the Real, Rilke in storm
> erecting a temple within
>   the ear.

Invitation to the Rose

He doesn't think you should do those things to a flower. Blooming innocently, verging on the virginal, head dew-filled and so lustrous it recalls the glow of adolescent skin. That light flushed pink, flesh-filtered, emanating from within.

She doesn't think you should do those things to a child. Pick any one and observe how, in a vase, as in a portrait, the subject expires. For years she's watched this happen. Again and again, the rose burns a hole in the middle of her page.

III

Crown of Roses

Postcard from Lesbos

It is written that in antiquity a visitor
to her island would have the tomb
pointed out. But there is no mausoleum
now no grave as there are no whole volumes
of her verse though there are words
though there are shards

buried more deeply in secondary sources
than the scrolls sifted from the sands
of Egypt. At the end

of the twentieth century, in Mytilini, what
I find is a statue in a square
of the southern waterfront. An altar
of cement in rubble, some straggly
flowers where the figure of Sappho
looks out to sea. Her Troy is
gone, Turkey darkens the horizon
and the port smells of petrol and piss.

She seems so bland, the muse, white-
washed by scholars into
                              immaculate
mother. As with the mounds of knucklebones
in the archaeological museum which tell
me nothing
              of hands, not whose, not how

many, this pasty icon is mute. What
remains of Sappho
                         besides a name,
besides a few lines without a face?
This milky model of a woman with her lyre

balanced on her shoulder like a jug is, if
mother, then mother of us all.

If Stone Dreams

We cannot know this statue, this satyr
with his head propped on a wineskin;
we cannot know if he dreams. In fact,
none can know in spite of aeons

of looking, of examining where his hip
is eaten away, eroded as if by our eyes.
For what has been lost we are to blame,
for what has been kept to be thrown
away. He sleeps, his brow furrowed, lips

furled, he sleeps in drunken stupor and his snores
though silent still insist. The need to be
drunk, we share this need to let consciousness

go. Satyr is the mentor
of blackout. He is the Bacchus we worship

within us. Observe in time his beard has grown
into the jug as man and vessel merge.
Together they seem content. He sleeps
because the wine has been drained.
There's no more stress, nor straining for he

no longer feels his hip, his brain, this unbearable
lightness. Now stone
seems to embrace this hallowed notion
of *empty*, of emptying space, this erasure, this sage
trace we sometimes leave behind. He is both

absent and present, a fading figure in a picture,
familiar, yet unrecognized,
                                    ourselves at another age.

Notes from the Blue Seas Hotel

1

Cicadas stridulating, calling back
Aurora, in ancient Greece, goddess
of transition, goddess of entrance
without performance. Of disappearance.
To love her is to love your youth & to
eschew your present age. I am
not what I was

        and fear what else
I may become. If it's not death this drying
up like tomatoes in the sun, this pickling
in the skin's own salt,

        what is it? Without the body,
a seed rattling in a painted gourd.

2

Though her love's infinite,
your body, alas, is short-
lived. No lover, no myth
no immortal can support
such a tender fact. In pity
Aurora transformed the breathing
corpse of her beloved into
an insect, a cicada which sings
most shrilly when she's not
around. In the high heat of August
Tithonus chirrs like an electric
drill. I have to turn on the air-
conditioning to shut him out.

3

This afternoon in the dawn
of the 21st century, taking a towel
off the clothesline, my hands
brush a whirring, a cybernetic
singing, a cross between a violin
and a blender, an organ
grinder with his pet
monkey on speed. I see

                    you, Jiminy Cricket,
wishing on a star, winged like a moth,
and your song rasping like a respirator.
Bug, as ugly as you are, still you can
claim in music more than immortality

you who know
                    what it is to have been
loved!

Makaria

You were called *Blessed, Makaria*, Lesbos,
isle of olives, green gold and grapes,
your wine redolent with flowers.

                        Flying in
the aerial view is more or
                        less what I dreamed.
In a silver jet with Apollo
emblazoned on the cobalt tail
                        fin might I see

differently? Might I then penetrate beneath the traffic
racing across asphalt-paved streets, override the revving
of engines and our modern reverence for motors,
to where

                        the ancient city, Mytilini
sleeps, to the very moment when Sappho
has briefly set aside her lyre? Hear
her call across the courtyard to a friend. Swish
as she fluffs up a silken pillow whose bright saffron
is muddied where the girl rests her yellow hair.
A voice undulates through the thickening dusk,
come, Sappho calls out, *it's late and I am word-*

weary. You and the rising moon will complicate
for the world the pallor, the pitch, of night,
richer in shades than any colour. More certain
than in alchemy, let's watch
                        blue become violet,
gold become platinum
                        as the moon's shadow
always casts
                        more deeply than the sun's.

Crown of Roses

I think that someone will remember us in another time.
— Sappho, trans. Jim Powell

*

Through centuries, through continents
the poet searched for a woman to tell
her story, for a time, a place, beyond
        the reach of Apollo's curse —

*

glukupikron, gluku . . .
sweetbitter, sweet . . .
close to me, her voice

                    because birds sing

in Greek . . .

                    because I'm listening . . .
                                        Sappho —

*

Goddess, didn't you promise me
that she who runs from me
would soon run after me,
that she who won't accept my
gift will then just have to

have it? are you fed
up with the favours I keep
asking because at your
altar I tune my lyre?

*

Some (men) say it's a team of players,
                    boys bent at bat their buttocks
harder than hard ball,
                    some (men) say it's a military band,
brass and shining,
                    the groan at the trombone, the groin,

some (men) say it's a fleet of jets,

heavily muscled with long-
range missiles which
                    is the father of beauty

but Sappho says it's what
                    ever you desire.

                    *

I worshipped Aphrodite, not Apollo.
You heard me sing ahhhhh . . . her name fragrant
as honey-clover in the steps of the reaper
          and not she . . .

my love left me for another face less
hideous, although my voice
in the lyric, at the lyre was sweeter
          than the breath of meadows

high in mountains where snow
runs into wood flowers, flora, fauna,
my ruin that spring, her fragrance, her
          lips at my lips

until she snipped the blossom for that bloke,
a husband. O all my prayers were blocked,
this time unheard by the love goddess, but He
          came because the verse

was passably *beautiful* — inadequate word — and
grave because a woman's pleasure dies
when the man desires. "You,
     Sappho of Lesbos

your name will be immortal, your verses
acclaimed into innumerable millennia."
But as you all know, the gods must be
     thanked. I was a fool

and cried out, "What good is fame
to me tomorrow when love stops
up her ears today!" I offended Apollo
     who cursed me after his blessing.

"It was a mistake," he declared (oh for a god
to err), "to offer a female a seat
in our august company. Henceforth let all
     poets be male

and though you have already entered
the eternal, like Tithonus, you will
not age well. What was radiant light,
     the silver of the moon

you sang and the world received as
newly minted, will become tarnished,
what was sublime, what was shining
     will become dross!"

*

. . . hair the colour of chestnuts
was the first thing to fade
ashes, ashes, stirring, sifting
        what remains of fire

and I who always shunned Hades
for the rape of Persephone must
linger by his gate. Sifting, stirring
        what remains of fire.

*

Centuries later another god arrived and His
high priests liked women even less than
did our deities who were not celibate.
        A Christian bull,

a medieval pope, condemned my poems
to the fire,
                            ashes . . .

                                                    ashes . . .

Sappho is not seraphim
Sappho's supreme
sin was to love
                women!

*

. . . on scraps of papyri . . .
sifted from the sands of Egypt
                            immortality
. . . my words not
            my mouth —

*

Time to come, marine
O wind, O wind, redolent
with the sea, with the salt
and iodine scent of sand
and dulse. Tell me will green
eyes ever again seem
                    so pungent?

*

A face pale as celery, my
pallor betrays me, my knees
knock at the door of an empty

house, no, not empty, but
sleeping, no, not sleeping,
locked in love's (not mine)
                    legs.

*

Your Lesbos is thousands of miles
and millennia from Montréal, this
March where snow fills the spruce
        like a mother shushing

her children. Is that your voice in the viola
or the weight of icy white in branches?
    melody or merely memory —

yesterday trilled in sunlight
robin, common sparrow and chicka-
        dee-dee-dee . . .

*

A pope, not a Michelangelo
virus, screwed up your text,
but these fragments lend
to the postmodern, you

                        have found your era,
Apollo has failed to
                        erase your future!

            *

whether at Cyprus
            or Paphos
                        or Panormus . . .

whether in Toronto
            or Ottawa
                        ou à Montréal . . .

the tenth muse will find you . . .

            *

                        . . . phantom words, not the mouth,

not the embalming of

            lips that I desired

*

That men are made
                    equal to the gods
by the love of women
(not by the phallus)
                    is true and you

worship when he bends
                    his knee, his foot
is webbed, you're wed
                    to a feather boa
a bird, a snake,
                    his beard, a beak,

the thrust between the thighs
                    and our sighs

weary, wasted, the god is in the beast
                    the best
man does not marry the bride
and from what feathered commotion
beauty, Helen and her twin, the white
        rose was born!

                    *

So some of my songs survive
merely in translation I must
thank Catullus for reincarnation
        in yet another male

voice! I was not Lesbia,
        but Lesbian.

                    *

Bless you Gertrude, but if
a rose is a rose is a rose is still

red, then it's not blank,
it's not blanched, it's not mine.

*

Brain children are all they can beget
so with such uterine envy the bearded
bard looks at the woman as her lyre
        leaps with a double life!

*

The anthropologist George Devereux called Sappho a
"masculine lesbian" with a "clinically commonplace
female castration complex"; if we were to adopt the Freudian
language we might add that his was clearly a case of male
projection and fear of the power of woman, the poet who
renders the word as flesh, not the flesh as wordy.

Q. How do you define "anthropologist"?
A. An apologist for men.

*

Why so dumb for so
long to open your big

mouth now? Don't you know
a woman's words should be

written in air and running
        water?

*

What is called history, testimony, in the literature
of men is called confession in the writing of women,
women who admit in print they're female, they're
        flawed, their fault.

*

I was not the only woman writing in my age.
When Corinna, with her verses, conquered
Pindar, the event was judged to be a beauty
        pageant, not a literary competition.

Among the lyric (I invented it) poets I was
declared the best, I must have been
to be lauded, to be loved, in spite of this
        face hailed as hideous!

*

My daughter, like your Kleis, yellow-haired
forsythia, broom in bloom, jonquil, crocus,
daffodil and narcissus, her headband
        crocheted lace

she bought for herself at the Gap
because I couldn't find one to match —
because even laurel could only be
        eclipsed by her curls,

this morning freshly shampooed
        and smelling of apple pectin.

*

Do not prattle like Praxilla . . .

                                    poetess —

*

The gods got it all wrong!
I wanted my daughter —

                        not my verses —

to be immortal!

*

Don't you know your dress thrills men
but me more. I don't care
                              if you ever take it off!
The way your gown, its soft linen
                              cloth clings to your hips

with the smoothness of marble
                              but oh, warm to the touch.

That colour becomes you
                                   shade of hyacinth
crushed underfoot, their fragrant bleeding
                                   or hue of grape
        foaming in Orpheus' cup . . .

The virgin is inviolate
                              the bride must wear violet.

        *

Why is it always Aphrodite's fault?
                              Who is really to blame
that I wasted my words (so they said)
                              describing fashion,
but tell me how could I,
without numbing the senses,
                              forget to mention
her sandals were gold lamé
                              and braided at the back!

*

The moon is half
                    full (or half

gone) the moon is round,
                        stoneground, a peasant loaf

sweetened with golden corn,
                        mealy and moist,

a peasant loaf when divided, when devoured
                                at the feast for which
you arrive too late.

Hunger makes even crumbs glow
                        brilliantly as wishing

stars. In the dark the moon
dazzles more than the sun
                        (for which we feel less need)

all night long Sappho
                    I also sleep alone . . .

            *

I do not expect
                to touch the sky

which comes down to earth
                        to touch us

with its anatomy of mist, with its digits
of rain, lonesome, in Montréal, in March,
it's all icy
            fingers; I sense the muse
through sleet and silence. Sleeping
in spruce, even the birds
                    dream only of you.

*

Bone, unlike bond, may not be torn, may not
be tattered . . .
                    ashes, ashes,

Know Sappho now . . .
                    in dust . . .
                                        in cinders . . .

                    *

Her tongue in my mouth
                    is eating anise . . .

                    *

Words are of air . . .
                    but they're shaped
in the mouth,
                    tinctures of the body

saliva and menses —
                    urine and faeces —

traced through each orifice, the oral —

whatever it is the body wants
whatever it is the body wastes

                                        not . . .

                    *

I was not golden, not a canary
or a finch, but a drab bitty
bird hidden under dusty

wings as if
                    flight itself, the sky could
                                        not be reached

by me. I had to fail,
though my song was a kite
unfurling its turquoise

eyes of the peacock's tail.
I had to fail, though your guy's
no poet, but a partridge

in his feathers, a parrot in his
screech! How could you dismiss

                              my music for him?

                    *

In love I was a figure of fun, taunted
as short, dark and ugly. Olive
green was my complexion, olive

black and heavily salted was my hair.
Some women's sandals adorn their feet,
but my calluses, corns, and bunions

begged for cover. Shoes always pinched
but you, Gongyla, beloved minion
of Aphrodite, your feet embellished

the leather they touched. To be trod
took on new meaning, to be trod
under your foot was to be

caressed by the goddess,
and Lydian braid against your skin
made silk look like clumsy, childish

corking. But immortality won't be yours
if, instead of me, you love (pathetic) him.

*

From the sands of Egypt, a column of
papyrus, stripped from a scroll, just
the middle, no beginning, no end
either. What it feels to be

                         incomplete.
What a woman's words are worth
when used to mummify a crocodile.
For millennia thanks to my poetry
                    the reptile is preserved.

He is still whole though I am ripped

                         apart yet my signature is
fresher —
                    Does this make me arrogant?

              *

Beauty is beauty
as long as you're looking

but goodness is more
than in the gaze,

such is consolation for the constant
Sappho who loves you

who sees right through you
to what you are, to what you will

become, each age, each phase,
a form of flowering. You are both

the blossom and the apple
tree in Aphrodite's orchard.

You are the seed, the boll
and the harvest! Natural

beauty is more than what
men admire, it's what

you take away, it's what
takes you away.

                    *

Can wisdom be gleaned from
aphorisms? The thin-skinned apple
when it becomes bruised fruit makes
wine without a (proper) vessel,

its sugar, its sweetness
                    turns sadder, turns cider.

                    *

If nobody believed that goodness was
better than beauty in a woman then
you can be sure nobody believes it
now wisdom is what . . .

                    *

when beauty is not skin
                    deep it is skin
wide . . .

*

A chalice of sky
a goblet of wine —

dark sea or my hand empty
and cupped, your supplicant,

all these elements, air, water,
and earth in its nocturnal blazing

with desire:
in the body all —
become fire.

*

This is the lover's discourse,
it needs no object, it offers
pure sign.
What? Who?

Why does Sappho love
since Atthis deserts her?

*

I was not always great
though I was called Sappho.
I often fed on sour grapes.

When I described Atthis
as small and graceless
as a raisin left on the vine,

even then I would have picked her
over all the succulent and dew-dappled
apples in Aphrodite's orchard,

even then I would not have
spit the pitiful thing out!

*

Sappho was **the** poetess.
Homer was **the** poet;
his subjects were heroes,
    their battles

their Mediterranean cruises and that war
waged against Troy for which the lovely,
the lethal, Helen was a petite
    pawn,

a tantalizing toy. Like the Trojan horse
she was full of the men who wanted her!
My style was not epic, but epithalamium,
    songs about who loved best

the bride and what the bride
wore: sandal, gown and braid.
That was news to the boys
in 571 B.C. —
        is it still news?

    *

. . . not lovely (Sappho)

        . . . loveless (Sappho)

. . . not happy (Sappho)

        . . . hapless (Sappho)

    *

pale waxing moon
a pool . . .

        of muted . . .

you're blind to . . .

        burning at noon

My daughter is golden like your Kleis,
I wouldn't trade the Mona at the Louvre
nor all the Simonettas of the Uffizi
        for her smile!

"Oh yeah, mom, that's what you say to impress her! If that were
really true! Then why did you drag me to the National Gallery
in Ottawa when all I wanted was something real, something
edible? Yummm, those beavertails, soaked in lemon and sugar!"

                *

In grade four my daughter built
our dream house in papier-mâché —
six inches wide, six inches high,
painted blue . . .
                        ashes . . . ashes . . .

Let it be my resting place,
Let it be my eternity box,
                        after I'm dead I'll fit

right in after I'm dead
I'll fall into
                        . . . ashes, ashes

and fragments
                        of bone
                        of home.

                *

From the back I took that boy
to be the bride
not the groom, the liar,
now I understand why she
left me for the lovelier.

*

I let Cupid use my lyre for his bow.
So all my music was tuned to our lord
of desire and my poetic practice was
pierced by the sharpest of arrows, the one
which shoots out to hit

directly within.

*

blood . . . burns . . . a temple
in her honour . . . ask not
to know what

ashes . . . ashes . . .

*

As incense scented

vanilla and strawberry

when the girl enters
the room is virgin

the room ignites

merely to smoulder.

*

Shall I compare thee to a wooden match?
which with the slightest scratch flames
up, yellow and blue. So briefly blinding
in the night, you burn, you burn
fast. I don't dare to stop seeing
you, though I should

drop you not
to singe my fingers!

*

You'll find me still among the pickers
where, though I am very hungry, I can
only watch. You are unlike any other,
you are the sweetest Manzanilla, you
are the one reddening, ripening, high

on the highest bough. After harvesting
they pack the apples, lift and heave the
weight of bushels, load them onto carts.
All these apples look alike except for
the windfallen, bruised fruit, half-
fermenting, odour of cider vinegar, offering
something for the nose though the bouquet

has withered for the eye. But you,
you're different, you can't be reached,
so you set the standard for red, for redness,
for beauty in fruit which can't
          be tested, be tasted.

                  *

Even in the insect world
there is music,

there is the poet, there is
the cicada, immortal

because of love
                  because of singing.

*

A dried-out husk, the corpse
of a cricket, the shell is all
that will be left of that man
after a hundred
                    hours with you.

I must send — not garlands, but —
wreaths to your wedding.

*

Helen strolled along the battlements
in the evening around and around
the city walls to keep her figure
trim. Though all Troy's torches were doused,
        her yellow hair was unquenchable

so that aiming by its aura the Greek archers
never failed to hit their targets — those happy,
hapless, love-drugged night guards, glad
        to die for her.

*

Exile in Sicily made Sappho sad
though the broom was in bloom
and Etna was steaming,

shooting luminous flares,
sparklers to hail all
her friends in Lesbos,

that community of women,
all, Sappho knew of love — all
she ever wanted to know.

*

It's not the years
but all those eyes
which wear beauty
out so a paragon's
face does not age

        well . . . well . . .

*

It's small comfort
for me as I am
used to losing never
having held the queen

        of hearts in my hand.

It was spades, spades,

        lucky Sappho,

in work, not in games,

        not in love.

*

Now that I nap in the afternoon I am not
above dreaming of your parasol, my unfreckled
hand held up to shield your azure eyes
    from the sun making you

squint. Who do you love now, Dika? Do
you doze as deeply with him? Does that
woodsy, wicked apple brandy you favoured
    still glaze your lips?

This glistening I imagine must be some sort
of illusion, its light like the moon's, its source
from something else. But what does it matter
    if she lights our way?

*

You always knew how to enjoy a lover,
whether crayfish or lobster, the shell has
to be cracked, you said, it's impossible
to love and stay
                    whole.

*

It's hard for an ordinary woman to
compete with the stars in beauty
but you, oh you could play body
double for the goddess,

when Aphrodite strips
off her robe, it's for you
all eyes ache.

*

What did you expect from wedded love,
girl? Regularity means eating oats every
night. Sappho says marriage is no fun —
        it's funeral for desire.

*

. . . as mother said when I was a girl
if you comb back your hair too tightly
into a ponytail, it will cut off the
            circulation to your brain!

which explains a lot about my friends —
why they line up to accept in marriage
the first dude who'll ask them!
        Just you wait,

mother said, just you wait,
it'll be the same for you!

*

Fame for fifteen
            minutes now

our gods offered
            forever!

    *

Tell the paparazzi Sappho says
wealth and beauty without virtue is
a woman
           without a purse —

    *

Not in art, but in the art
world if it's genius, if it's genuine
Picasso, it's not painted,
                it's minted.

    *

What happened, Dika?
Did the goddess
           plant
a garden in your mouth?
O kisses
           tasting of dill.

    *

In your presence it is more than
possible to pronounce petals,
though not so eloquent as the folded
        message of your musk rose.

*

Waiting for the moon we have wilfully
talked all night to prove the tongue
touches more deeply than his
          finger. Come now

let's stretch our legs, let's stroll
down to the river and listen to
dawn, to our sun rising again
          for the very first time.

*

When I was a child I was not
a child, I was graceless . . .

                    I was guilty . . .

*

Too bad there is no rose

                    without the aphid!

*

In the dark the perfume of diminutive white
flowers, lilies-of-the-valley, is as aromatic as
forests, in the dark the eye of the mind dims
          as the body stirs —

*

Earth with her many garlands
is embroidered and you
weave bright yarn in your walk,

the brightest woof of light and flesh
moving, you make me shiver from
head to toe, not from cold, though I feel

chilled, then hot, then chilled again
though it's not winter and that's not
an avalanche shaking the ground

as you approach the air's so sweet
I thought the hay freshly mown
and sky raining flowers!

*

When the pigeons' spirits grow cold they let their
wings droop at their sides, flight is forgotten.
When a mother abandons her child, unloved
the waif wraps her arms around

herself as a vine around the body of a flower,
as if to struggle towards the light as if
to survive were to strangle.

*

For me
neither the honey
nor the bee.

But for the lover
of men the stupid
stinger.

*

You daren't look dowdy in downtown Montréal
promenading along St. Laurent
where lipstick is a trope, a jazz note, red
red lips, *partout c'est*
        le rouge!

*

I saw a wan face or was it the moon
above wisps of clouds, her downy
tendrils, her highness, her hair forever
    unmanageable, my rosy-fingered

goddess, now tagged a satellite with footprints
and flag planted in her sands. Sappho says
you are a moon, Maria, you shine more
    brightly before a man stakes his claim.

*

Touch, oh touch of your hand, cool,
no, your lips on my brow and O
this fever, this so-called
        life without you . . .

*

It upsets you when they don't all
adore you, Sappho, and that even
with professed love, there's a pinch

            of something else,
            of something less.

*

Of all the senses touch is not
diminished by aging. Touch
treats the skin as Braille, lines

form the texture of text,
wrinkles are resonant, the richer
verse in your visage. Some find

their pleasure in the latest look, in the book-
of-the-month, but mine's intent on rereading
        you, my beloved classic.

*

It was Ovid who wrote me as a figure
of fun. A cunt. It was Catullus
whose flatteries were his sincerest
        works, to Lesbia, all

imitations of my lyrics. I do not count
men my enemies as I count
(almost naively) women my *bosom*

                              friends.

*

Even homely as honey-clover
I like best the smell of white
        flowers which sadly

can't be had without the help
of the drone, that slothful bee
        with his furry back leg.

*

... and words had for me the delicacy, most prized,
of flowers, of the rose, its petals many-layered, its heart
opening fully to take you inside, its scent, its pollen, its
        sex making you sneeze!

*

When we die we close but
temporarily we are
what morning glories

trace in dusk, their
brilliance, furled, their scent
blind in the backyard.

*

In the script, in the score, the dead
speak more loudly than the living,
their music plays on. You must
        attend at the graves

of such as Sappho (if you can find it),
of Sylvia, of Caruso or Chopin
to listen, as if for the first time, to the strains
        of their silence.

*

Though it is possible to be

              immortal and some

say I invented this for poetry

              the woman in her words

laments her age

              is not less.

    *

The rose preserved is different
from the rose fresh, the rose
preserved in poetry or potpourri
must have all her petals

              pressed.

    *

The doctors prescribe

              estrogen replacement therapy

the rich inject

              placental tissues and medical miracles

in Rome a woman gives birth

              to her granddaughter.

It has been promised to those

              entering the 21st century

that they may never leave . . .

              that they will always live . . .

*

At the back the bee is armed
but up front honey
is what she regurgitates.

She is a true *femme*
fatale who can placate
with sweetness or
                    stun with her stinger.

                    *

Now that she's gone back to
her husband,
                    I make do with herb
tea, plain. Now I desire the un-
adulterated,
                    unlike her crack-
ed cup which can't be filled.

                    *

Yes she calls him honey
in the morning, but who
gathers the bee's cloying

confection, who bakes the bread,
who brews the coffee, who
slathers toast with sweet

whey and why does it always have to be . . .
her heart fueling the hearth? and
                              for him?

*

For the young, age is just a number,
but for me, whose eyes no longer
see what's nearest, what's dearest,
     whose myopia has moved

into denser fog, into mystery, so that even this
note in your hand, saying *yes! meet me as planned,*
I must hold at arm's length to read. The page
     is blurred. The hand never rose

up again to wave goodbye from the funeral
pyre. I thought I'd see you again, my friend,
when I returned from Sicily. Your farewell,
     smiling, the cancer, a mere

blemish on your cheek. Ask not for whom
the cards are dealt. Ask not for whom
the bluff is played. Was it remission or
     permission? Your last words to me:
                         Or I'll come to see you!

*

Behold Bronwen's ashes. At the threshold
of her fame, she died, though she remains
in literature where her spirit is a bird
     caged in song, a song

without singer. She was like you, Sappho,
a muse, in the new world, a poet who
found her art in her friends, girls in glasses,
     quick with quotations,

gossip and grace. Let's cut off our long hair
to lay our curls on the grass growing over
the grave of a feminist. Like you she was
     plainspoken, but not so sarcastic.

*

We made the night
                last twice as long
but eternity
                we could not
extend beyond
                do you remember
when?

                *

From a bone fragment they can reconstruct
the whole animal, a giant and ancient
        lizard, the dinosaur,

from bits of burnt paper, from quotations
in other texts, what is made
        of my voice, stutters, hic-

coughs — they can recreate the body of a dragon
but the woman at her lyre remains a phantom —

you must listen for what
                I have yet to say —

Sappho on Ovid

If nature denies me the gift of beauty,
  let my name's measure be my stature.
  — Ovid, *Heroides*

Shall I send you greeting? Do you recognize
  Sappho's voice? Though no bones ferry
back from the river Styx, words still may fly
  to you from the other side.
                    Through a love
letter Ovid penned in my name, my life was
  falsified. He distended my lyric
mode into the lofty, marmoreal lines
  of his elegiacs, subverted
the style to have me confess (unlikely) lust
  for Phaon, the proper male lover
for whom Sappho must let go all those tender
  names: Anactoria, Gongyla,
Dika, Atthis, Cydro, Iranna . . . I loved
  and cursed. Without them my fingers were
ever untempted to pluck a string! For what
  but to woo them! I never knew shame
in love though I blushed from uncertainty, spite,
  resentment and jealousy, bitter
salts to disguise when meat's bad. But Ovid's source
  for this verse was Attic comedy
wherein I'm married to *Kerkylas* from *Andros,*
  (in English, Prick from the Isle of Man).
Because my poetic rank could not be touched,
  they dragged in my status as a wife.
To win laurels men wrote for the gods
  about war; while I wrote for the girls
about headbands, of Lydian design, threads
  of bright gold woven with indigo.

In this fiction of my marriage I only
  delighted in duty, in guilt-free

love, a husband's, and in a daughter's sweet
        devotion, until I was blinded
with desire for Phaon. Such a fool as I
        have been for no man, if for every
other woman!
                In his own time Ovid was
called impure, exiled to the Black Sea for *Ars
        Amatoria*. The empire banned
him from the world of the Latin tongue. So did
        he need a poetess, a scapegoat
to deflect from his art, his own infamy?
        My subject, the heart, was his object.

Among immortal gods in the *Heroides*
        I alone step in from history.
As an insipid figure of fun! But my
        dispute is not with Ovid alone,
it's with you, scholars, critics, readers
        and all who continue to believe
the big lie, the heterosexual one —
        millennia of misogyny.
Where is the philosopher's so-called logic
        when a woman's involved? Tell me what
woman would prefer words of war to words of
        the wedding? Or would choose elegies
over epithalamia? I hear her
        yes, me, through lips stained pomegranate.

        Ovid's words were rags soaked in kerosene,
stuffed into my mouth — in flames, Sappho, the torch
        singer. Sappho fawning over some sailor.
That was not mine, that was a man's point of view,
        his pawned off as *hers*.
                        What's dignity
worth for Ovid to claim I deferred the crown
        of laurel to Alcaeus who was
from Lesbos too and my contemporary?
        What's dignity to any woman?
a dip in the ink-pot for the poetess
        who often dipped in rouge to welcome

all her loving(ly) (reluctant) readers?
     What is dignity but a well-heeled
sandal? In fine leather the tone never slips.
     Can you believe I elevated
Alcaeus above myself? No doubt he was
     the better man, if not the greater
poet. It's men who enshrine men, prefer tomes
     according to their own standards. Deep. Deep
throat of drinking-barrel they esteem, along
with a warrior's breaking wind, not the lilting
     lyre, not the tortoise shell that sits
so smoothly on the hip of the poetess.
     What, me, praise those dirty ditties of
battle above singing? Were I reborn male
     I swear I would embrace falsetto!

Where's male logic when a woman is
     invented? Phaon, Ovid's creature
was my gigolo rowing a gondola
     across what must have been the Lethe —
its waters like Alzheimer's making me
     forget my genius, my girls for the boy
only briefly beguiled by the poetess
     strumming on her aging instrument.

Beauty of the muse is a temple erected
     for the ear, but a sty(e) to his eye.
Beauty of the body is not ethereal,
     but muscle and musk. There's no essence
in sex, there's scent, O there's singing at every
     orifice. But do you suppose such boys
are born to sit and listen? Not in life, not
     on this sacred earth would I desert
my pretty maids, my dew-filled roses, to lie
     with pine needles up my backside. But
he could tempt Mars — so Venus dared not touch him.
     That's a more likely detail in Ovid's
story, such beauty in a boy might attract
     me as I adore the feminine

wherever it can be found in the body.
       But, to neglect the fairest flowers
for him, to shun their silken corollas for
       the sting of the stamen? To forget
their brilliant hues for his bilious beige, his bald
       head? To tear my garments, my garlands,
strewing the petals for Phaon to step on?
       When Ovid took up my pen, he chose
the woman of straw. Inquisitors love to burn
       the sibyl, to drown the witch's speaking
in silence. Throw myself off cliffs for some kid?
       Forget the fragrance of white flowers
and drop the pudendum for the dusty, dangling
       spores of the pod? Bad enough to lie —
worse to show me as a pathetic matron
       ready to dash her brains out for some brat.
Sappho grovel for a guy, she who never
       grovelled for a girl! Yes, the lie is indeed big,
big enough to be believed by all. Implausible
       though the tale, when male logic records
something in female history, what is not
       blotted is left out. Blank. My epistle
in Ovid's *Heroides* is more full of holes
       than a harem, than the ten volumes
that held my verse.

                   That high place, the stormy cliffs
       at Actium where it's said I leapt
into the sea, was so remote from Lesbos
       to get there would have meant voyaging
through all the Greek isles or, even more risky,
       over the mainland. On the advice
of a nymph. If I had survived the pirates,
       the plunge into the ocean, I would
have been as old as Odysseus! So was
       Phaon a wife, a Penelope
to wait for me? to shun all other suitors?
       What funeral could interest a boy?
tempt the roving eye? or lure anybody

away from new loves? Among all of Ovid's
mythical characters, I was the living
    woman, the writer, the real witness.
It's ironic how the only way to kill
    the heart and not die is to keep
the massacre on the page. The water nymph
    promised that his Sappho would triumph,
that she would float right up as her gloomy heart
    plummeted into the depths to drown.
It's Ovid's version of this absurd story
    that deserves to die along with *his*
Sappho. I was no suicide. For the vegetable
    god, a dirge was all that I ever
played on the lyre for Phaon. I served

Aphrodite above all. My self, my singing,
those scrolls, offered to love in the feminine.

Stanzas for Sulmo (Sulmano)

*

I wish I were a girl in Sicily
            on my lips was blasphemy.
Would Ovid whine that way
            for his own exile, to be beached
again at the Black Sea,
            out of reach of the beloved
hills of Sulmo, glittering
            with grapes and goat droppings?

*

My poetry made me immortal
            and my name still gives Phaon
breath in the story Ovid wrote
            I am no longer joyless and dry
though the boy forgets
            Sappho as soon as he picks
up his clothes, he forgets
            what heat, what words, can do.

*

If indeed
            we toiled at the task of love
you know
            the man was no
boy or the boy
            was no man.
I always had good
            reason to prefer women.

*

Her face, more radiant

       than Phoebus whose name

means *shining*,

       blinds me to a thousand

and one others.

       More heliotrope than human,

without shame,

       I still watch, I still wait.

Acknowledgements

"Crown of Roses" works intertextually through quotation, improvisation, and parody. The primary texts, Greek and Latin, were used in English translation. What follows is a bibliography of primary and secondary sources for this work on Sappho:

Balmer, Josephine, *Sappho, Poems & Fragments*, Carol Publishing Group, 1993.
Barnstone, W., *Greek Lyric Poetry*, Indiana UP, 1967.
Carson, Anne, *Eros the Bittersweet*, Princeton UP, 1986.
Greer, Germaine, *Slip-shod Sibyls*, Viking, 1995.
Isbell, Harold, trans., Ovid, *Heroides*, Penguin, 1990.
Powell, Jim, *Sappho: A Garland*, Farrar, Straus & Giroux, 1993.
Whigham, P., trans., *The Poems of Catullus*, Penguin, 1974.

*

I would like to thank the University of Rome for an invitation to visit as writer-in-residence in May 1991 and External Affairs Canada for funding and supporting my stay in Italy. This facilitated my visit to Duino and then later enriched the writing of *"La Benvenuta."* I would like to thank Concordia University for an equipment grant as well as a sabbatical travel grant for my trip to Lesbos, summer 1996.

The epigraphs and a more general debt are owed to Leonard Cohen and Gertrude Stein. *"Répondez s'il vous plaît"* is indebted to Baudelaire as well as to Rilke's poetry (mostly in Stephen Mitchell's translations) and letters.

I would like to thank Kim Maltman and Roo Borson for their reading and suggestions, their encouragement and interest in this work along the way. I would like to thank Sharon Thesen for sending me Jim Powell's translation of Sappho to cheer me up. And *Arc* magazine and P. K. Page for choosing the selections from "Crown of Roses" for the Confederation Poet's Prize 1996.

But my deepest gratitude as well as many garlands are due to Erin Mouré for her brilliant and generous editing of this book.

Some of these poems have been previously published in various forms in journals: *Arc, Border Crossings, Canadian Author and Bookman, Fireweed, The Montreal Gazette, Prairie Fire, The Fiddlehead, The Malahat Review,* and *Matrix;* in the anthologies *BITE TO EAT PLACE: An Anthology of Contemporary Food Poetry and Poetic Prose,* ed. Adolph, Vallis, and Walker, Redwood Coast Press, Oakland, California, 1995; *Border Lines: Contemporary Poems in English,* ed. A. Wainwright, Copp Clark, 1995; *Making a Difference,* ed. S. Kamboureli, Oxford UP, 1996; *Prose Poems and Sudden Fictions,* Moosehead Anthology #6, ed. Allen and Loewen, 1997; *Take This Waltz: A Celebration of Leonard Cohen,* ed. Ken Norris, The Muses' Company, 1994; and in other versions in *Stranger in You: Selected Poems and New,* published by Oxford UP in 1995.